HANK BROOKS

MATCH MAKER

Gay Romance Erotica

WARNING

This book contains sexually explicit scenes and adult language. It may be considered offensive to some readers. This book is for sale to adults ONLY.

* * * * * * * * * * * * * * * * * *

Please store your files wisely where they cannot be accessed by underage readers.

Please feel free to send me an email. Just know that these emails are filtered by my publisher. Good news is always welcome.

Hank Brooks – **hank_brooks@awesomeauthors.org**

About the Publisher

4Fun Publishing, a member of **BLVNP Incorporated**, 340 S. Lemon #6200, Walnut CA 91789, info@blvnp.com / legal@blvnp.com
NOTE: Due to the highly emotional reaction of some people to works of erotic fiction, any email sent to the above address that contains foul language or religious references is automatically deleted by our anti-spam software and will not be seen. All other communications are welcome.

DISCLAIMER

Please don't be stupid and kill yourself. This book is a work of FICTION. Do not try any new sexual practice that you find in this book. It is fiction and not to be confused with reality. Neither the author nor the publisher or its associates assume any responsibility for any loss, injury, death or legal consequences resulting from acting on the contents in this book. Every character in this book is over 18 years of age. The author's opinions are not to be construed as the opinions of the publisher. The material in this book is for entertainment purposes ONLY. Enjoy.

Match Maker
Gay Romance Erotica

By: Hank Brooks

ISBN: 978-1-62761-795-6

Part One

This is really going to sound strange, so read slowly, and let it all sink in. My father is gay, very gay. I am straight, as straight as one can be. My dad has never hidden his sexual preference from me. He has often brought men home, and after getting me settled in bed, he would invite the men to his bedroom.

He always closed both our doors. It didn't matter. As I grew older and recognized the sounds of love, I knew full well what was going on behind those closed doors. I didn't have to be taught to respect Dad's privacy, I did it out of natural common sense.

What's that? You don't find that too way out? If it were a question of vice versa, it wouldn't be so way out at all. Well, let me add, that I am not adopted, nor am I a foster kid. I am the natural son of Maurice Pierre LePont, Sr., actually descended from French royalty. His friends made fun of the fact that he was a real *queen*. I didn't get the significance of that double entendre until I was almost an adult. I would have been insulted for him, but I knew it was said in jest.

Let's explore the situation even more. There is no mother in sight. I never knew her. Are you curious enough yet to want to know how this all came about? How did a gay man have sex with a woman, and conceive me? Whether or not I have piqued your interest, I myself became curiouser and curiouser when I was about fourteen years young. I was determined to ask my dad about it, but I wanted to wait until the right time. The right time was a long time in coming.

One evening, shortly before my eighteenth birthday, we were spending a quiet evening at home. My dad did not have a visitor over that night, and I decided not to hang out at the mall with my friends. We were sitting side by side on the living room sofa watching TV. We were both wearing cargo shorts and nothing else. I don't know about my dad, but I had nothing on under the shorts.

"Dad, I have something to tell you."

"Shoot; fire away," he said with a smile on his face. He lowered the sound of the television set with the remote control, which he always held in his hand, throughout an entire evening of watching TV.

"I had sex with a girl last weekend. I'm not a virgin anymore."

My father tried to act blasé, but his smile betrayed him. I could read the pleasure in his face.

"Say something," I begged.

"I hope you used protection."

"Of course. I'm not a dummy."

He put his arm around my shoulder, and pulled me tightly to him. "Well," he said, "at least we know which team you play for."

"For sure, but the reason I'm telling you all this is that I wanted to make you realize that I'm not a kid anymore. I'm an adult, and I want to hear your story. I want to know how I came to be, and what kind of a relationship you could have had with my mother. I have a right to know."

My dad looked stunned, but he peered into my eyes and said, "Of course, you have the right. I'll begin at the beginning."

He shut the TV, leaned back on the sofa and began.

***

"I was a couple of months shy of my college graduation, and I was at a gay bar with my trick du jour. (Dad was never shy about discussing sex with me...maybe because he was gay, and I'm a guy). On the way out I picked up a couple of gay magazines. Those rags are mostly filled with business ads and I didn't usually bother with them, but I did this time, and I took them home with me.

"I was glancing through the ads, and I came across an eye-catcher. Some lesbian, named *Maria*, was seeking to purchase sperm from a donor, and she was offering a thousand bucks to the right guy. Boy, was she specific. The guy had to be six feet tall, or better. He had to have strawberry-blond hair, green eyes, a short nose, a square chin, no excess weight, a flaccid five-inch schlong, or better, and it had to be cut. Can you imagine all that? I don't reckon that she got many answers to her ad."

"But, Dad," I interrupted.

"I know. It sounded like the ad was written for me, so I called the number in the listing. She wanted to meet me, so we met for brunch the following Sunday. She sure as hell shocked the socks off me, Maury. She was gorgeous, but she hit me between my eyes. She declared that I was perfect, but that she had more to demand of me. These were demands that she couldn't put in the ad."

"Wow! What were they?"

"I had to marry her. She had to prove to her co-workers that she wasn't a lesbian. She felt her career was being hurt by her sexual orientation. When the baby was born, she said we could divorce and I would sign over all parental rights to her, so that I didn't have to pay any child support.

"She went on to say that we had to be seen places together during the pregnancy. She also said she would not mind if afterwards, I had some presence in the child's life so that it could have a male father figure, even if the father was gay.

"I told her that was above and beyond the parameters of the ad, and I would not do it for less than twenty-five hundred dollars. We settled for two thousand. I was still a student, and I really needed the money. As soon as we shook on it, she told me that her real name was Marianna Gallo. She was a real Italian beauty, your mother was."

"I guess things didn't turn out as expected," I mumbled.

"No, they did not. As soon as her pregnancy, by artificial insemination, was confirmed, your mother and I had a civil wedding down at the court house. We began to do things together and we found ourselves enjoying each other's company. We both particularly enjoyed theater, opera, and ballet; well you already know what I like. She liked it too. We became really good friends, and we were not rushing the divorce.

"Late in her pregnancy, she shocked me. She wondered if I would like to move into her spare bedroom so I could help her in the early days, and be a father to you.

"That's when I surprised myself by saying yes, but only if she promised that I could have 'company' occasionally. She said that she had no objection, so I agreed. This is the very apartment, Maury. We've both lived here all your life."

I sat motionless. So where was my mother? What happened to her? I needed to know. I didn't want to ask directly so I merely muttered, "Yes, yes, please go on."

"We actually lived like a married couple for about six months, except I had visitors over, and your mother did also. When you were about a week shy of your seventh month birthday, I noticed a change in your mother. She began to lose too much weight. Her appetite disappeared, and I couldn't get her to eat. There was no color in her cheeks, and I begged her to see a doctor. She poo-pooed me.

"One evening she collapsed at the dinner table. I called 911, and to make a short story even shorter, she was diagnosed with acute leukemia. She was gone in two weeks. Maury, I didn't realize how dear she had become to me. I was devastated. It was you, and only you, who kept me alive. You became and still are, the focus of my life. Thank God, I had a good job and could afford to hire help and nannies."

I sat still. The silence was offensive. Dad realized that he had to lighten the mood. "I love you so much," he said, "that I don't even give a fuck that you're straight." He broke out laughing, and there was nothing I could do but laugh with him.

A few days later, my father asked me if I was still seeing the girl who took my virginity. I said yes, and we were going at it pretty regularly.

"Good," he said. "I'm making dinner Friday night for me and a *friend*. Would you like to invite your girlfriend? We'll have an intimate little dinner party."

"Then what?" I asked in a bitter tone of voice, that wasn't like me at all. "You two will go into the bedroom, and I'll have to explain it all to Wendy? No thanks. I need to figure out when and what to tell her, if we continue to see each other."

I could tell my dad was really hurt, but he said with a smile, "Well maybe another time, just the three of us."

"Yes," I said, "that'll be a lot better."

That Friday, Dad had his dinner party. I had been pretty harsh on him, so I decided to stay home that evening, help him prepare dinner, and meet his friend. I started to think about it. He had actually invited me and Wendy to dinner with this guy. I began to imagine that whoever he was, my father might be developing feelings for him. I had always believed that maybe I stood in my dad's way of having a relationship with anyone.

Then I realized that in just a few months, I would be off to college, perhaps never to return as a member of this household. The thought of it chilled me, and I couldn't imagine what that was doing to my father. He'd be all alone, an empty nester.

When I realized how imminent our parting was to be, I decided to do the gayest thing I knew. I was going to be a match maker for my father. The problem is, I knew my father's two or three close friends, but I didn't know any gay men who might be a suitable match for him. I certainly didn't know how to go out and find one.

I decided to tell Wendy that my father was gay, and to seek a woman's advice in the match making game. She thought the whole idea was cool, and couldn't wait to meet my father.

"Place an ad in the personals," she suggested.

How obvious. How dumb could I have been? If the ad were for me, I would have used Craig's List. I knew my dad would never go to that website, but I hoped a prospective boyfriend would. That way, he probably wouldn't be older than my father, and more likely he'd be younger. I spent several days tweaking the posting. I was never satisfied, but I settled on the following, which appeared one weekend later under men seeking men:

Tall, strawberry-blond, and handsome. Thirty-something. Not into one night stands. Seeking to meet like-minded guy for possible long-term relationship. Let's enjoy all the performing arts together. Religion and race are not factors. Please E-Mail maury2@ gmail.com. A picture would be an extra added attraction.

I attached my father's Facebook profile picture to the ad, and prayed. If I was gay, I'd sure be attracted to him. My mother knew what she wanted, and he had passed the test.

On Friday evening when the doorbell rang, our guest was ten minutes early. My dad was in the bedroom preening. How gay, I thought with a smile, and went to answer the doorbell. I was pleasantly surprised. The good looking guy standing there was about ten years older than me, and ten years younger than my father. I couldn't help being happy for my father, but when I realized that I was sizing up a dude, I grew frightened. I better not be turning gay, I thought. After all both my parents were gay. It could happen.

"You must be Maury's son," he said with a smile, which looked more like a leer. He thrust a bottle of wine at me, and stuck out his hand. "I'm Gary."

"Pleased to meet you, Gary. My dad should be out of his room any second now. Throw your coat on the bed in my room, and have a seat in the living room. I see this is white wine. I'll put it on ice, and be back in a jiffy."

Gary looked a little surprised. I don't think he thought that I would know that white wine should be served chilled. Hey, I live in a gay household. I let the good stuff sink in.

While I was in the kitchen I thought to myself that my dad must be one hell of a lover to have snared this good-looking younger guy. Because of our different sexual orientations, we had never really had the 'birds and the bees' discussion. Maybe I should pick my dad's brains after all. I'm sure it would translate well to straight sex also. Certainly, he wouldn't be shy to speak to me about sex.

Our apartment was very small, and our dining room table only sat four people. I sat on one side with Gary, and my dad sat facing us. Our appetizer was grapefruit halves with a cherry in the middle. I told Dad to sit, and I served the course right out of the refrigerator. As soon as I sat down, I got a real shock. Gary placed his hand high up on my thigh.

The SOB was coming on to me!

I neither moved nor reciprocated, but when I stood to remove the grapefruit dishes, I made sure that I moved my chair so that it was somewhat out of his reach. My father was serving the London broil with roast potatoes, and Gary kept smiling at me. I averted my eyes from him, and certainly I didn't smile back. It was all I could do not to panic, but I did make a plan.

"After dinner, Pop," I said. "Just pile the dishes in the sink. I'll load the dishwasher when I get back. I'm meeting some of my friends at the movies. You and Gary just relax and have fun."

When we finished our dessert, I held out my hand to Gary. "It was nice meeting you," I said.

"I'm really sorry you're leaving us," he said, sounding genuinely disappointed.

I had no idea what I would do, but I had to get out of the house. I figured I would really go to a movie. Of greater concern to me was whether or not I should tell my father about Gary's tion. Maybe he just assumed I was gay, and he might have thought that I was fair game. He could even have had a threesome in mind. I just shuddered and ran to the movie theater.

When I got home three hours later, I expected to see Dad's bedroom door tight shut, and sounds of love making coming from behind the closed door. Not so. Gary's coat was gone, and my dad's door was wide open. He was lying in bed and reading from an electronic device. I was surprised and pleased. Thoroughly Modern Maury, I thought.

"Where's Gary?" I asked.

Dad smiled and said, "Let me tell you something that's a universal truth, whether it has to do with gay sex or straight. If a booty call is just that, a booty call, and there are no special feelings, then it's never an over-nighter. If feelings are developing between two people, it often becomes a sleep-over."

"That's good to know, but also not so good to know. I've never known any of your 'friends' to stay overnight. I'd love for you to find a partner, Dad. I'm not going to be around forever."

"I'd like that too. Maybe Mr. Right is just around the corner. I just haven't met him yet. Now you get to bed, and stop worrying about me."

I wasn't finished yet. "I'm glad you don't have special feelings for Gary. He was trying to feel me up under the table."

"I know. He thought you were a gay boy toy. He didn't believe you were really my son. He told me that he was disappointed when you left. He was hoping for a three-way."

I broke out laughing. "That'll be the day. God night, Pop. I love you."

Part Two

I could not believe how many responses I got to my ad. I think my mailbox was filled to capacity. I closed myself in my room and started to review them. I was in there way too long, and my father wanted me out of there stat. I told him I was working on a term paper, so he finally stopped bugging me.

The first thing I did was to eliminate every response that didn't include a picture, or had a nude picture attached. I was left with only twenty-one letters. I thought that next I would eliminate anyone whose picture was not appealing to me, but I changed my mind. Since I was straight, I figured I wouldn't know what would appeal to a gay man. Instead, I began to read the little blogs. At first I was appalled. The writers would describe in pornographic, explicit language what they would do to, and with, my father. I almost vomited.

When I came to the fifth letter, I nearly cried. I liked the look of the writer as well. He said he was 5' 9". That was small next to my dad's 6'1". He also mentioned his weight, and I calculated that he was slightly overweight, but he had the jolliest face. His blue eyes sparkled. Thank God, he didn't describe his cock and its dimensions as the others had. I liked him just from his picture, but his letter brought me to tears.

Dear Maury2:

I guess we are about the same age. I'm thirty-five. I cannot remember a time when I didn't know that I was gay. In my youth, I erroneously believed that a gay man could never find the same deep and enduring love as a straight man, but I did. His name was Michael. We met one night in a gay bar. It was love at first sight. We had two great years together, but Michael was an army reservist. He got called up, and was killed in a roadside ambush in Iraq five years ago.

Since then I have been like Elton John's Candle in the Wind. My existence is tenuous, and I survive with moments of happiness, and hours of misery. The happy times come to me from my students. I teach history in a local high school. The relationship I have with my kids keeps me going, but I am so, so lonely. I can't bring myself to hang out at the bars, so when I read your ad on Craig's list, I thought, what a wonderful way to meet someone, and see how things go.

If you are willing, I'd love to meet you in some public place, and get to know you. I am so lonely, that even if you just wanted to be my friend, I would be grateful.

Hopefully,
Eddie Morgan.

I e-mailed Eddie immediately. I told him what times I was available to meet with him, and asked him to get back to me with a time and place. I believed that it would be best if I met him somewhere, and told him that my dad knew nothing about this. I would then play cupid, and set up a 'chance' meeting for the two of them.

Five minutes later I heard from Eddie. He told me to meet him on Friday, at 4 PM, at a certain diner. I wrote back that I couldn't make it that day, but I would be available the following Friday. The truth was that Friday was my eighteenth birthday, and my dad was planning a special day for us.

Eddie wrote back and confirmed the following Friday, and then I started a different search. The diner he chose was right next to my high school, and Eddie said he taught at a high school.

I looked up my school on the web and clicked on staff. Sure enough there was a brief bio of Eddie and his picture, obviously taken a few years earlier. I was pleased that Eddie didn't lie about his age. He was three years younger than my father. I was never in any of his classes, and I was sure he didn't know me amongst the thousands of kids that attended this heavily populated city school.

I went into the diner a few minutes before the appointed time, but I didn't take a seat, and I refused one when the hostess wanted to seat me.

"I'm waiting for someone," I said.

I spotted Eddie immediately after that. He looked so nervous, that I wanted to embrace him and reassure him.

As he came through the door, I approached him. "Are you Eddie?" I asked. "I'm Maury." He looked at me long and hard.

"Why would you lie like that to me? You're jail bait. Are you trying to entrap me?"

"Oh, God, no," I cried. "I'm Maury Jr., and I'm not jail bait. Please let me explain." The hostess came over and asked to seat us. I took Eddie's arm. "Please," I said, and we followed the hostess to a table.

"What's going on?" he asked. "I'm really not amused to be made a fool of like this."

"Please," I said for the umpteenth time. "Order something, and I'll explain."

"Fine," he said in resignation.

Without going into detail about my father's contract with my mother, I just told him that my mother died when I was seven months old. "My father raised me, but he also realized that he had been living a lie, and reverted to his gay lifestyle. He so devoted himself to me, that when I go to college in a few months, he's going to be alone and lonely, and maybe fall apart.

"Please forgive my little subterfuge," I begged. "I only did it to make my father happy, and hopefully you too. Your letter touched my heart."

Eddie smiled and we both relaxed for the first time. "Is your father as nice as you are, and is he as handsome as his picture?"

"Yes sir, he sure is. And just so you know, I'm straight."

"Thanks for telling me, but you're way too young for me, anyway. I'm definitely more interested in your father. You say he doesn't know about any of this. Have you hatched a plan for us to meet 'accidentally'?"

"Not yet. I was hoping you could help me with that."

Part Three

"Have you eaten?" Eddie asked me.

"No, I haven't."

"Will you let me take you to dinner and we'll talk?"

"Great."

I took out my cell phone and called my dad, who didn't swer. I left a message telling him that I had baseball practice and would be home late. I added a P.S.: "Don't hold supper for me."

"This diner is all right for lunch and quickies, but there's a great restaurant just around the corner," Eddie said. "We can walk over. It's a little early. I'll have a cocktail, and I'll buy you a coke."

"I'm not old enough to drink in New York, so I'll settle for the coke."

We got a table and had our 'cocktails' there. Eddie told the waiter we would order when we finished our drinks.

"I've decided to be blunt with my father," I told Eddie. "I'll invite you to dinner, and I'll tell my father up front that I wanted you two to meet."

"How do you think he'll take it, being fixed up, I mean?"

"He's unbelievable. He goes along with anything I want to do."

"OK then. When will you invite me?"

"I'll clear it with my dad, but how does next Friday strike you?"

Eddie started to laugh, but the laugh was bitter. "I thought I made it clear to you that I'm a very lonely man. My calendar is really a blank any old time."

"I'm sorry," I said.

"It's OK. Now that we have that out of the way. Let's just talk. Ask me anything you want to know about me."

"Eddie, I find you so easy to talk to. My dad and I talk freely about our sexual orientations, but there are a few things I've always wanted to ask him about, but I didn't have the nerve."

"I take it you would like to talk to me about it. If yes, shoot. Frankly, you honor me."

"Have you ever had sex with a woman?" I asked, shocking Ed.

"Sadly no. I've always known that I was gay. Have you ever questioned being straight, and thought about sleeping with a man?"

"No."

"Do you know if your dad ever had sex with a woman after your mother died?"

"I have no idea. I never asked him."

"You're beating around the bush, Maury. What do you really want to ask me?"

I decided to come right out with it. I waited a long time for this opportunity, and I didn't want to blow it. "I can't imagine two guys making love to each other," I started out. "Women are so soft and curvy, so desirable. How can you even get turned on by a man?"

"Good God, Maury. I wish I could answer that question. It's the secret to what makes me gay, and what makes you straight. Since I'll never sleep with a woman, and you'll never sleep with a man, I guess we'll never be able to compare."

"You've got that right," I said, but I wasn't convinced in my own head. After all, when all is said and done, I was a curious teenager.

"I just don't get it," was all I could muster up to say.

"You should give it a try once, just to see what the fuss is about?"

"Ugh! I don't think I could."

Eddie laughed so hard, I thought he would choke. "Then you'll never know the joys of gay sex," he said. "Maybe you should try it just once, so you can compare. I'm a good teacher, you know."

Two emotions swept over me as I considered his offer, curiosity and revulsion. "Would that effect how you feel about meeting my dad?" I asked in all sincerity.

"Hell no, I want you to know the joy your dad feels when he has sex with a man. I promise it will only be a one-time shot. If you want more you'll have to go out and find it elsewhere."

"Let's go for it," I blurted out. "I could come over to your place tomorrow morning."

"No. It's now or never. If we wait until tomorrow, you'll change your mind. I need this more than you. I live walking distance from here. Let's go."

We never did order dinner.

Part Four

When we entered Eddie's apartment I was shaking like a leaf. I really wanted to chicken out and run, but I didn't. My father loved gay sex, and obviously Eddie did too. I reasoned that one time wasn't going to turn me, and I would have the opportunity to experience what gays do together. I mean I know what they do, but only in my imagination. In reality, I might not enjoy it. It might even gross me out, but I could chalk it up to sexual experimentation, and forget about it.

"You're as white as a ghost," Eddie laughed. "Relax. Nothing I do will hurt you. I promise it will make you feel good." He enveloped me in his arms.

"You're shaking like a leaf. Come with me." He led me into his bedroom. His strong arms still encircled my shoulders. He took a picture from his dresser. Two smiling young men had their arms around each other, just as he had his arms around me now.

"I'm going to pretend that you are my late lover, Michael. Believe that, and know that I only want to give you the most pleasure I am capable of, in the same way I gave it to him."

I don't know why, but somehow that did calm me down a tle. Eddie took his arms away from my shoulders, and started to remove my tee shirt. Some instinctive force made me help him, and soon I was naked from the waist up. He was wearing a sport shirt. He started to unbutton it, and I helped him to take it off. We were now evenly naked.

"Sit down on the bed," he ordered in a seductive voice. I did, and he began to remove my sneakers and then my socks. I watched him as he kicked off his shoes and took off his socks.

I assumed that he would then undo my belt, and pull down my pants and underwear. Never assume. He laid me gently on his bed, on my back. He crawled on top of me. I could feel his hard cock pressing on my flaccid one. I can honestly say that I wasn't revolted, but I was plenty scared. I wondered if I would even get an erection. I didn't wonder long, because I got my first dose of eroticism. Eddie's tongue was licking inside my ear.

I was dumbfounded. His tongue was sending electric currents through my body, and I was feeling it in my prick. I felt myself swelling. Somehow, I came down to earth. Wendy had never done that to me, but it wasn't disgusting, and if I asked her to do it, I knew she would. Hell, I would do it to her first.

Electric jolt number two happened when Eddie moved down my body and started suckling my nipples. I never knew how erotic it was to have my nipples sucked like that. I realized how much I was enjoying this, and I panicked, until once again, I realized that a woman could do this to me as well. So far the experience was not too bad, but not enough for me to opt for gay sex over hetero sex.

For sure now, I thought Eddie would go for my belt. I was wrong again. Instead, he placed his lips on mine. I wanted to turn away, but he tightened his grip and I couldn't. I gave into his kiss. I pretended it was Wendy kissing me. When he sensed that I was relaxed, I felt him part his lips, and then his tongue brushed lightly against my lips. I don't know why, but I parted my lips also and our tongues met. For a brief second I pretended I was still with Wendy. Little by little, Eddie's tongue was transporting me to another world, a world where Wendy disappeared, a world populated by millions and millions of Eddie's.

Nothing made any sense to me. Someone whispered in Eddie's ear. It certainly wasn't me. "I'm ready," the phantom voice said. I expected Eddie to surely remove my pants now, but he didn't. He jumped out of bed and started to remove his pants instead. He wasn't wearing underwear. While he was doing that I thought that he had teased me enough, and I took off the rest of my clothing.

Eddie stood over me smiling. His cock was long and thin and circumcised. It was longer than my cut one, but I was heftier. He put his cock near my nose. For whatever reason, he wanted me to smell it. It smelled sweet and scented. It wasn't what I expected. Actually I didn't know what I expected.

He got back in bed, and straddled me once again. He began to kiss, or I should say, lick his way down my body until he reached my innie. He renewed his suckling. This time his target was my navel. I began to squirm, not because I found it erotic, but because he was tickling me. He sensed I was uncomfortable, and continued his downward journey.

His nose and lips nested in my pubic hair, and I could feel his tongue licking the area. My thick, wiry hair did not seem to deter him. By now, my cock was throbbing with anticipation. Hell! No guy, straight or gay, is going to stop anyone from giving him a blow job.

"Please," I whimpered, and he took me. At first he just ran his tongue up and down the underside of my shaft. He was teasing me in the most pleasant way. After a few strokes, he took my balls in his hand and started to fondle them. Occasionally he licked them. As he was doing this, his fingers were running up and down my ass crack. When he did that I began to lose my senses. I squirmed and whimpered, but Eddie didn't stop. Suddenly, he took my entire cock into his mouth and at the exact same moment, he inserted a finger up my ass.

I had never felt like this before. The double whammy of my cock being sucked, and my ass being massaged, was just too much. I knew I would blow, and blow hard, and blow soon. Eddie knew also, and he pulled off and out of me. I whimpered again, and he said, "Patience, my little virgin. Better things are coming."

Why did he call me little? I was at least three inches taller than he was. I wasn't going to get mad at him for something so petty. I wanted my sexual experiment to move on.

"Before I let you cum, little one (little again), you must taste my cock or it's no experience at all." He placed his cock on my lips and I turned away.

"If you give up now," he said kindly, "you'll never know the joys of gay sex?"

"I suppose you'll want to fuck me also," I said facetiously.

"Of course," he smiled, "but not before you fuck me."

My stomach turned when he said that, but my 'ugh' moment was short lived. Suddenly I realized that I did want to experience it. I never wanted to have to say in later years, "I coulda, shoulda, or woulda."

I wrapped my hand around his pulsating cock. It felt so strange to hold another guy's rod in my hand. I could feel its inside hardness, and its outside velvety softness. I put it to my lips. I gave his piss slit a tentative swipe with my tongue, and captured a bead of pre-cum. It really had no taste at all.

I licked his shaft, as he had done to me, and then, using all my resolve, I took his cock into my mouth. He was so long that I could only manage to swallow half of it. I continued to lick his shaft, and finally I began to play with his balls. His balls began to harden and his breathing became labored. He pulled away from me. I found myself being unhappy, and I grew angry at myself for liking this too much.

He jumped out of bed, and I was overwhelmingly disappointed. I needn't have been. My teacher was ready for my next lesson. He removed a box of condoms and a tube of KY Jelly from his drawer. "I hope these rubbers are still good," he said. "I haven't been with anyone since Michael was killed five years ago."

"Then why use them at all?" I asked.

"What about you?" Eddie asked.

"Wendy and I took our virginities together, and we are monogamous. Well, we were, until this minute."

Eddie smiled, and tossed the questionable condoms aside, and reached for the lube.

"Lie on your back," he instructed me. I had begun to soften, but when he began to stroke my cock and bathe it with lube, it hardened right up. I couldn't help thinking, that until now I was certain that I couldn't be aroused by a man.

He put a good deal of lube up his ass, straddled me, positioned my prick at his crack, and began to sit on it. He winced a few times as my fat cock entered him, but when it was all the way in, he sat perfectly still, sighing with delight.

"Does it hurt?" I asked

"A little at first, but the ecstasy far outweighs the momentary pain. You'll see." I wasn't sure I wanted to find out, but I had committed myself to experience the full range of gay sex. I was sure there was more to learn, but I figured that my teacher was teaching me the basics.

Eddie started to move his ass. "As I push down," he said, "you thrust up."

I hardly heard him. Wendy's vagina was never this tight nor so well lubed. We depended on her natural juices. So far, this was the first gold star for gay sex, and the first strike against hetero sex in this whole experience. Until now it had been pretty even. I could do all that we had done thus far, with a woman also. I had no trouble sucking on a clitoris instead of a penis. In fact, I preferred it.

Eddie continued to move his ass up and down my cock. I had never in my life felt anything so sensual. Neither my own hand jobs, nor

Wendy's vagina, ever affected me anywhere near this way. I felt a strange tingling in my toes, like they were being stimulated by an electric current. The current began to spread throughout my whole body, but instead of being warmed by it, I began to shiver. My whole body quaked as I yelled out, "I'm cumming."

Eddie stopped moving, and I pushed my cock as far up his ass as I could, while shooting stream after stream into him. I could feel my own cum reversing direction, and begin to leak out of Eddie's ass.

He leaned over me, and we started to kiss. By now I was enjoying his kisses. Besides it seemed a natural thing to do after an orgasm. Eventually my softening dick slipped out of him, and he rolled over to lie at my side.

"Your cock was doing a good number on my prostate and I almost came," Eddie said. "I was able to keep myself in check, but I tell you, Maury, I need to cum badly. You could jerk me off, or suck me off, but I think you need this final experience to feel what your father feels. Let me fuck you."

"Yes, yes," I muttered.

Eddie placed a pillow under my butt, and reached for the tube of KY Jelly. He told me to raise my legs, and he squirted a good amount on my crack. He inserted one finger and began to spread the jelly inside of me. He removed his finger, took another glob of the stuff, and inserted it with two fingers. It didn't hurt me, but it was uncomfortable. He started to ream and stretch my opening. Suddenly a wave of pleasure swept over me. One or both of his fingers had rubbed against my prostate gland.

I gave out a little cry of pleasure, and Eddie smiled. As I told you his penis was long and thin. He lubed it real good and placed it at my crack. He entered me rather easily. There was a twinge of pain now and then. He began to fuck me in this missionary position. His cock was massaging my prostate, and I thought I might cum again. I am at a loss for words to describe the euphoria I was feeling.

I did cum again, and when I did, my ass constricted. Eddie screamed like a banshee as he spurted several massive doses of cum up my ass. In this position very little oozed out. We lay quietly like this for a very long time. Eddie lay on top of me, and our lips met once again. I could not get enough of his passionate kisses.

Finally he rolled off of me. "Well?" he asked.

"I have to admit that I had fun. You taught me a lot, Eddie. I can apply some of these things when I make love to Wendy, like kissing her inside her ears, and suckling her tits longer, and her belly button too."

"I didn't get to it before, but try sucking each of her toes. I promise you, she'll love it." He scooted down the bed, and demonstrated on my toes. My cock started to rise again.

"Was there anything you enjoyed the most?" he asked me.

"Yes, the feeling I had when you fucked me."

"Yes, yes," he agreed. "Don't you think that it's awesome that God placed a sex organ in a man's ass? It proves to me that he meant for men to be homosexual, and to use women only to procreate."

"That's an interesting theory. I'll have to think about it. In the meantime, I can understand why gay men enjoy their sex so much, but I would still rather hold a woman in my arms."

"I'm glad for you," Eddie said sincerely. "It's much easier to live life straight than gay."

"I want to thank you for this experience," I said. "It was way beyond fun, but we need to talk about you and my dad getting to meet each other." I was going to say, getting it on together, but I thought better of it. It might be a bit premature.

"Let's not wait another whole week," I continued. "My father and I work out at Gold's Gym whenever we can. We're going there this Monday after he gets out of work. We usually arrive about 5:30, work out for an hour or so, and then we hit the showers. There's a nice diner right next door, and we usually have dinner there before heading home. Could you be there at the gym? I'll introduce you as one of my teachers, and ask you to join us for dinner. Sometime during the workout, I'll whisper in my dad's ear that you're gay."

"That's no problem at all. I have a membership at Gold's. You can bet I'll be there."

"Eddie," I said, "my dad is never to know about this little encounter. I may tell him someday, but I'll decide if and when."

"My lips are sealed."

"And Eddie, thanks again. You are a good teacher. You taught me plenty."

Part Five

When my dad and I got to the gym, I looked all over for die. He had arrived before us, and I spotted him on a treadmill.

"Hey dad," I said smiling broadly. "There's one of my favorite teachers on that treadmill. Let's go over there. I'll introduce you." I lowered my voice and whispered in his ear. "He's gay, you know. Everyone likes him. He's very popular, so don't be shy with him."

"If I didn't know better I'd think you were trying to set me up."

"I would have said 'fix' me up. No matter. It wouldn't be such a bad thing after all. Would it?"

As we approached Eddie, he spotted me and smiled. He slowed down the treadmill and stepped off.

"Hi Maury," he beamed over me. "It's so nice to meet you outside of school walls."

"Sure, Mr. Morgan. I'd like you to meet my dad. He's Maury, Sr." The two of them shook hands, and I was encouraged by their smiles.

"Call me Eddie, Maury, Sr."

"OK, if you drop the senior."

"It's a deal."

"The treadmill next to Mr. Morgan's is available, Dad," I pointed out. "Why don't you take it and I'll take that one over there."

My father smiled at me and whispered in my ear. "You *are* try-ing to fix me up, you scamp. You've got good taste."

Eddie and Dad went together from one piece of equipment to another. I think they lost track of time, so after about an hour, I inter-rupted them. "Hey guys, it's time to quit." I turned to Eddie. "My dad and I are having dinner at the diner next door. Would you like to join us, Mr. Morgan? We'd really like that."

"Sure. It'll be a pleasure."

We headed for the showers, and boy did those two check each other out. There was no subtlety employed whatsoever.

My father has more nerve than anyone else I know. Right in the middle of dinner he took Eddie's hand and said, "My son told me that you're gay. Did he tell you I was also?"

Eddie broke out laughing. "Yes he did."

"He's trying to fix us up, you know," my dad smiled at Eddie.

"Well, if he is, I'm a very compliant victim."

"Me too," my dad said. "How would you like to come for dinner Friday evening, Eddie? Maury, you can invite Wendy if you would like."

For some reason I didn't feel like it would be wrong to have my girlfriend over with Eddie there. In my mind, he wasn't a trick. He was a bona fide guest.

"Sure," Eddie and I answered simultaneously. He and my dad were still holding hands.

"When will you guys be here at the gym again?" Eddie asked.

"Wednesday," I answered.

"Good, then I don't have to wait until Friday to see you again. Do you want to have dinner together after the workout?"

"Absolutely," Dad answered.

On Wednesday evening, Dad told me to go home, and that he and Eddie were going to hang out for a bit. He came home very late. I was still up and he gave me a big kiss on the cheek.

"Thanks," he said.

***

For whatever reason, Wendy insisted on helping out with the dinner. She came home with me right after class on Friday, and we got things going. My dad wouldn't be home for a couple of hours, and Eddie was told to come at six. This time I told my dad in advance that Wendy and I would be going to a movie right after dinner, and I would take her home after the movie. He would have private time with Eddie after we left.

"Are you sure you don't want to give us our dialogue?" he asked facetiously. I ignored him. I wasn't going to let him spoil my master-piece.

Everything had been prepared early that morning. This time I had four salads, covered with Saran Wrap, in the fridge. I popped the standing rib roast in the pre-heated oven. It too had been pre-prepared along with roasted potatoes and spices. An apple pie was in the fridge, and ice cream was in the freezer.

Wendy and I were so efficient that we had spare time before anyone came home. We started to make out, but I heard my dad's key in the door, and we separated quickly. It made me wonder if my dad would break his hold as quickly, if I came upon him making out. Well, I had no time to dwell on the matter. He said hello to Wendy, and told us that he needed to take a quick shower before Eddie came over.

It was obvious before, during, and after dinner that Eddie and my father were getting along great, but I had a terrible urge, which I had to restrain. I kept wanting to tell Dad what a great lover Eddie was. I guess that came from wanting to push things along. Of course it was pure folly and I knew it, but still, the urge to shout it out was with me all evening.

I absolutely felt a surge of warmth throughout my whole body when they started to make plans to attend theatrical and sporting events together, especially my next high school baseball game. Wendy felt my excitement also. She kept smiling at me.

After dinner, which got rave reviews from Eddie and Wendy, we all chipped in cleaning up. It was early spring and the nights were still rather crisp. Wendy and I grabbed our jackets, kissed both men good-night (me too) and went on our way.

Eddie and my dad had been together the previous Wednesday evening so there was no pre-sex awkwardness. I did learn sometime later, however, that on Wednesday they only had oral sex. As soon as we were gone, they were all over each other. As they began to strip, their kisses were hot and passionate. When they came up for air, Dad whispered, "God bless, Junior."

"Amen," Eddie whispered back.

"Let's go to the bedroom," Dad suggested.

"Yes, and will you fuck me please? I've had a five-year hiatus, and I'm desperate." Eddie almost blurted out that in all that time, he had only gotten fucked once. He realized, just in time, that an admission like that might raise questions. Eddie and I were having a tough time, keeping our little get-together a secret.

Not only did the two men, who were so dear to me, fuck each other into paradise, they also brought each other off with their tongues and their lips. Eddie wasn't going anywhere that night.

When I came home, their bedroom door was ajar. From what I could see, they were wrapped in each other's arms, fast asleep. Dad and Eddie were enjoying an over-nighter. I knew what that meant. I was elated. And then I got the strangest feeling. I remembered how it felt to get fucked by a man in the ass, and I got jealous. I wanted it too. I was shocked and appalled at my thoughts. I closed their door and went to my bedroom, where I jerked off trying to think of Wendy, but all that came to mind was Eddie's cock massaging my prostate.

Part Six

Wendy and I didn't have much in common except our mutual desire to have sex together. So when she went off to the University of Michigan, and I drove upstate to SUNY Binghamton, it was no great tragedy. I was the first of us to leave the nest. The afternoon before I left, I drove to Wendy's and we had bang-up sex. Unfortunately, I was still remembering getting corn-holed in the ass, while I was fucking Wendy in her vagina. I had to wonder if it was simply a memory, or if being fucked in my ass was becoming an obsession.

My experimental indiscretion had long since stopped being a concern to me. I had learned to accept that it happened. I refused to have regrets. I figured it was just a fantasy, a passing fancy, which I would eventually get over and forget about. I could not accept the fact that I might be having homosexual desires. It wasn't that I had any prejudices against gays. The two dearest people in the world to me, were gay. It's just that I refused to be gay myself. I cursed the day that I let Eddie talk me into having sex with him, *just for the experience*. The more I thought about it, the more I came to believe that he had seduced me.

So what the fuck. I really didn't care. Together, he and I had the best sex I had ever experienced. I asked for the experience, and I got it, in spades. I actually envied my dad. He and Eddie had become a couple, and he was getting from Eddie what I yearned for. Hell, how could I even think of cursing the day, when it gave me the best memories of sex I could ever imagine?

When I jacked off, I began to picture all the things Eddie and I did. The visions overpowered me, and gave me really intense orgasms.

By the time I drove up to Binghamton, Eddie had been living with us for a couple of months. I can't tell you how happy that made me. I could leave with the full knowledge, that I would be sorely missed by both my dads, but they would not be alone and lonely.

Driving alone on the New York State Thruway, I offered a prayer to whichever God was in charge of matchmaking. I prayed that in college I would meet my soul mate. We would get married, have kids, and make Eddie and my dad grandparents. Out of the blue, I allowed myself to wonder what would happen if my soul mate was someone with a big cock, who could massage my prostate. I immediately erased the thought, and went on with my drive.

The dorms were set up for four students to a room. One, or maybe two, of my roommates had arrived a day or two before me. The room already smelled sweaty. Dirty socks and underwear were lying on the floor. I knew then and there that I would seek off-campus housing for my final three years.

Only two of my roommates were slobs. The other one was a neatnik like me. His name was Joseph Barrie. He swore to me that he was a descendent of J.M. Barrie, the author of Peter Pan. I had to believe him. After all I expected him to believe that I was descended from French royalty. He was also a New Yorker, but he lived on Long Island and I lived in Manhattan.

Joseph and I did our best to keep our room clean and smelling nice. We used Glade products constantly. We became very friendly, and we hung out together. He agreed to move off campus, and to be roommates the following year. We figured we would start our hunt for a place at the beginning of the spring semester.

We were well into our first semester when something struck me as odd. Our other two roommates were dating and chasing pussy constantly, but neither Joe nor I seemed interested. We were both serious pre-med students, and I chalked it up to the fact that we really didn't have time for the pursuit of the almighty vagina. I figured that if I met a girl in the ordinary pursuit of my everyday life, then fine. But I wasn't going out chasing. I never discussed the situation with Joe and he never said anything to me. I was just grateful for his friendship. I didn't seem to be making any other friends. I didn't even try out for the baseball team. I was determined to focus totally on my studies.

Our lives turn on delicate spindles, and our destinies on rusty hinges. A seemingly unimportant event changed my life forever. It wasn't even something that happened to me, but it sure affected me.

Joe's father was a well-known surgeon, who had invented a revolutionary new surgical procedure. Dr. Barrie lectured all over the world, teaching his procedure. Months before, he had accepted a speaking engagement in Vancouver. As the date approached, he realized that he and his wife would be in Canada over the American Thanksgiving holiday. The harvest holiday was celebrated a month earlier in Canada.

When Joe said that he might not go home for Thanksgiving because he would be all alone in a big house, I immediately insisted that he come home with me. Joe happily accepted. About an hour later, I realized my mistake. I couldn't renege, so I decided to tell Joe the truth about my home life. If Joe could not accept it, then fuck him, for not being much of a friend.

I took Joe to an off-campus coffee shop. We found a quiet table in a corner, and I proceeded to tell him that my father was gay. "He came out after my mother died of leukemia," I told a little white lie. "He has a partner now, and he lives with us. You'll have to share a room with me." I started to laugh. "Just like we do now."

Joe was silent for what seemed like hours. I couldn't stand the suspense. "Aren't you going to say something before I go crazy?" I asked.

"Can I assume that means that you don't hate gays?" I thought that was a strange reaction to my momentous announcement.

"Of course not. I love my father, and I've come to love his part-ner."

"Are you gay?"

"Hell no. I'm straight," I said without conviction. I was having serious doubts.

"I have something to tell you, Maury. I've wanted to tell you since we met, but I was so afraid until now. I'm gay, and I hope you and I can remain friends, and that I can still go home with you for Thanksgiving. I'd like to talk to your father and his partner. Maybe they can help me come out. I could use some advice."

Joe's plea was pathetic. I embraced him and whispered in his ear. "We're friends, Joe, good friends. Nothing has changed between us, so stop worrying and let's plan our trip home."

The first thing I did when I was alone, was call home and request that my dads pick up a sleeping cot for my room. We only had two bed-rooms. I wasn't afraid of Joe attacking me. I was afraid of becoming inappropriate with him. I couldn't seek my parents' advice without pos-sibly disclosing the event between Eddie and me. I held that encounter dear to my heart, and I wouldn't do anything to taint it, or distress my father.

I also felt it appropriate that I tell them that Joe is gay. That prompted hours of conversation between them, regarding my own sexu-ality. Dad said, I had a gay friend because I was comfortable with it, after living with him all these years. Eddie said that he disagreed. He thought I had some homosexual leanings.

The next time we were in the shower, I paid close attention to Joe's endowments. Somehow I had never done that before. He was cut, almost as long as Eddie, and almost as hefty as I am. In short, he had a gorgeous cock. I felt my life getting more and more complicated. I was actually admiring a cock.

After Joe came out to me, I avoided talking to him about his sexual orientation. However, I didn't want him to think that I was disinterested, so one evening, when we were alone in our room and the others were out partying, I asked him if he had ever had sex with a man.

"I wish," he lamented. "It's all I think about, but I'm still a virgin."

Goddammit! I almost told him that I had sex with a man once, but I caught myself in the nick of time. Afterwards, I gave it some thought. Maybe I should tell him about the "experiment" and describe it to him, so if I should slip up in the future, he won't think I'm hiding my possible homosexuality in some closet or other. On the other hand, if I do tell him, he might slip up at home over the holiday. I decided to keep my secret a little bit longer, if not forever.

"Have you tried to meet any other gay men on campus? Isn't there a gay and lesbian coalition?" I probed.

"If I meet someone, then fine," Joe said, "but I'm not going out looking."

Shit! I had said the very same thing, but about a woman. I simply told him that I felt the same way.

We drove home on the Tuesday before Thanksgiving in my old Nissan Sentra. I prayed it would last through my undergraduate years. (The old war horse didn't give up the ghost until I was doing my residency at Beth Israel Hospital in lower Manhattan, many years later. Joe ended up at St. Vincent's, immediately across town.)

We were pretty silent on the trip home. I was absorbed in worrying about controlling myself when we were alone in my bedroom, and Joe was making up a list of things to ask my dads about.

We arrived at our apartment before either Dad had come home from work. I knew that Eddie would be home first. When he came through the front door, he practically broke all my bones hugging me so tightly. He kissed me on the lips, and Joe stood by in amazement. I figured my father would be more restrained. He had toned down his demonstrations of love for me, when I assured him that I was straight.

I introduced Joe to Eddie, who gave him a bone crusher as well. This time Eddie could feel Joe's hard-on, so he aborted the hug gracefully.

"I'm cooking, and making all the fixings for Thanksgiving dinner, so we're going out tonight as soon as your father gets home," he told me. "Do you guys have something in mind?" he asked.

"Chinese," Joe and I said simultaneously, and Eddie decided then and there that we were in love, if not yet lovers. We were exactly alike in many ways that only Eddie could discern.

"Take Joe to your room, Maury, and get him settled."

There was the cot at the side of my bed, neatly made up. Even at that, it was too close. I just knew I was going to weaken. We unpacked and hung our skimpy stuff in my closet.

I don't know what possessed me, but I blurted out, "In the dorm I wear boxers, Joe, but I always sleep nude at home. Would that bother you?"

After some hesitation, he answered, "No, that'll be fine. I might even join you."

I could have kicked myself. There was no need to make such a statement or to sleep naked.

We went back into the living room to wait for my dad. The three of us had just begun to chat, when my father bounded in. He kissed me in warm welcome. He wasn't holding back anymore, and I loved it. He held me so tightly I wanted to cry. Finally, I introduced him to Joe, and he not only hugged Joe, but he kissed him too. Joe loved it also. His father loved him, he was sure of that, but he never showed it and never embraced him.

At the Chinese restaurant, Eddie asked Joe if he was out to his parents.

"Yes. I decided to tell them before I left for college. I have an older brother and sister. They're both straight, so my parents won't miss out on the grandparent thing. They were OK with it."

Joe realized that Eddie and my dad might be sensitive to 'the grandparent thing,' so he said he was sorry about that. They smiled and my dad put his hand on Joe's.

"Is there something you would like to ask us?" Eddie asked.

"Nothing specific, but I'll take any advice you can give me."

"Well, the first thing I would advise you is to tell your parents, but you have already done that," said Eddie. "Don't be afraid to tell people that you are gay. It gets easier and easier every time."

"If you meet someone you are really into," my father interjected, "tell him up front that you're gay. If he's gay, you might have met your soul mate. If he's straight, and accepting, he might become your BFF."

Joe looked at me and said, "I've already done that also. I don't know where I stand yet, but I hope to find out soon."

"Yes," Eddie said. He looked straight at me. "Your friend should declare himself ASAP. It's not fair to keep you on a thin wire."

I was miserable. How could I declare myself if I didn't know where I stood myself? Joe would have to remain patient with me, or fall in love with someone else. I had no idea at the moment how quickly things would come to a head.

I had to lighten the mood, so I looked at Joe, and said, "These two guys are the noisiest lovers you ever heard. I'm warning you in advance, so you won't be shocked."

"I guess we want the whole world to know how much we love each other," Dad said. An errant tear appeared in my eye, and in Joe's. After that we concentrated on the delicious meal, made small talk, told jokes and had a great evening. Joe was like part of the family that night, and I couldn't have been more pleased.

It happened in the bedroom after we went to bed. It was a rare thing for me to do, but I closed my door. Joe and I stripped all the way, and I gazed at his beauty. In fact, I gazed, and gazed, and gazed some more. I didn't even realize that we were both erect.

I thought back to my evening with Eddie. Not only did I love the sex more than anything I had ever done with Wendy, but I began to have suspicions about myself. Maybe Eddie's gaydar picked up on it also. He couldn't make me or anyone else gay, but that night, he made me realize who I really was.

Now I stood gazing at Joe, realizing how much I loved him, and sensing how much he loved me. I started to cry.

"Fuck the cot," I said. "Sleep with me. I want us to make love forever. And Joe, if it's of interest to you, I have strong suspicions that I'm a bottom."

"That's nice to hear, but do you think you might be a lot more versatile? Ever since we met, I've been dreaming of your cum shooting up my ass."

"I promise," I said, "that if you'll be my partner, we'll be full partners. I'll do whatever pleases you, and I would expect equal treatment."

Joe didn't answer. He fell to his knees and took my cock in his mouth.

"Stop," I said. "There's something I have to do."

I grabbed a blanket to cover myself up and walked across the hall. My fathers' door was ajar. I peeked in, and saw that they were just climbing into bed. I knocked lightly. They weren't surprised to see me, but I kind of think my purposeful, determined arrival stunned them.

"What's the matter, son?" my dad asked.

"Er…" I hesitated, "Do you think I could borrow…might you have an extra tube of lube?"

Now they were shocked and surprised. My father started to laugh and to cry at the same time. They both rushed to me and embraced me, slobbering me with kisses.

"Your father owes me a hundred bucks," Eddie informed me.

"You bet on me?"

"Yes, I knew you were gay the night I met you, and we had sex together."

"Christ!" I said.

"Don't worry, son, I told your father all about it. I couldn't start our union off with a secret or a lie. He insisted that it was a one-time shot, an anomaly, but I said that I was certain that you were a gay man, struggling to come out of a straight body. Your perception of yourself as being straight was, to say the least, faulty."

He reached into his night stand and took out a tube of lube. He handed it to me and said, "We'll talk about this in the morning. Now go have fun and use some of the tricks I taught you."

I kissed both of them, and ran back across the hall. Joe was waiting for me in bed. He was naked and his erection looked huge to me. I threw the tube of lube on my nightstand and climbed into bed with my guy. We wrapped our arms around each other, and crushed our cocks together.

"I love you," Joe said.

"I love you more."

Part Seven

Joe rolled over on top of me. His warm lips touched mine, gently, like a feather. I started to shiver.

"Please," I murmured, "do to me what you want me to do to you, so I'll know exactly how to please you. Remember, I'm new at this."

"Yes, I know, and so am I. We don't have to rush. We have our whole lives ahead of us. All I want for us to do tonight is to hold each other tightly, fondle our cocks and our balls, and kiss. Your kisses are sweeter than honey.

"Next time we'll suck each other to Nirvana, and the time after that we'll fuck. I know how much you want me to fuck you, love, but I want to lead up to it. If we take it slowly, a step at a time, it will be all the sweeter."

Joe rolled over, and we faced each other. He took my cock in his hands and started stroking it so tenderly, I felt myself being hypnotized. I reached for him and started to do the same.

"Nice," he repeated over and over again.

It had certainly been an eventful day, and we both drifted off into a deep and peaceful sleep.

When I awoke, the dawn was just breaking and Joe was still sleeping. In spite of the early hour, I heard noises from the other side of the door. I needed to pee anyway, so I got up, and went out into the hallway. Eddie and my dad were in the kitchen, sipping coffee, and reading the morning newspaper. They were wearing robes, but I could see they had nothing on underneath.

"Well, there's our sleeping beauty," Eddie said. "Tell us all about it."

"There's not much to tell. I did want to meet someone special in college. I just never expected it to be a guy."

"Are you certain?" Dad asked. "I just don't understand how someone who has been straight all his life, who has fucked women, could suddenly turn gay. I know it could never happen to me in reverse. I fell in love with your mother, Maury, but I could never have sex with her, nor she with me."

"Please don't ask me to explain it. All I know is that I did fall in love with Joe, and more than that, I wanted to make love to him. It's as much a mystery to me, as it is to you."

"What's a mystery?" Joe asked as he entered the kitchen.

"Love," I answered simply. Joe embraced me and kissed me on my neck.

"The fact is," Eddie said, "we were musing on how Maury switched teams so unexpectedly. That begs the question; was he always homosexual and suppressed it, or was he straight, and his love for you caused the switch?"

"I can't answer the question," Joe said. He thrust his hips forward and motioned in the direction of his cock. "Now tell me gentlemen, wouldn't this turn any man gay?"

Everybody laughed.

"The only thing I know for sure is that Eddie and I have to go out shopping for our Thanksgiving dinner," Dad scolded. "Please get dressed and stop getting us all hot and bothered. He and I have no time for play. From now on, it's work, work, work."

Joe and I showered together. Back in my room, we waited until we heard my two dads leave, and we hopped back into bed.

"You promised that our next step would be blow jobs," I reminded Joe.

"That sounds just fine to me. Do you want to play sixty-nine or should we go down on each other one at a time, alternately?"

"Let's take turns," I whispered. "That way I can give my full attention to making you happy, without any distractions."

"I love the way you think."

"Let me do you first," I said in a very weak voice. My emotions were getting the best of me.

I didn't have Eddie's maturity, nor his patience. Without first exploring Joe's body, as Eddie had explored mine, I went immediately for my target. He smelled so good from our recent shower. I took as much of his cock into my mouth as I could, and used my tongue and lips to suckle him. I thought I'd be revolted, but his cock was like an aphrodisiac. I took more and more of him into me. I wanted to swallow him whole to show him how much I loved him. I felt his balls shrinking and hardening, and I knew he was cumming. Suddenly he pulled out of me.

"Fuck, I don't want to wait for the next session. I want to cum right now, and I want to cum up your ass, Maury. I love you so much."

I became frenzied. "Yes, yes" I squeaked, reaching for the lube. I squeezed some of it onto my hand and stuffed it into my ass. I was afraid that if I rubbed it on Joe's cock, he would cum prematurely.

I think Joe was as wild as I was at this point. I rolled over on my back for him. He aimed his cock at my ass hole, and ram-rodded in. Eddie had entered me very slowly, and did not hurt me like this. I was angry at Joe, but not for long. The initial pain and burning were waning very fast, and I felt the pleasure I had felt with Eddie. I dared hope that Joe's mammoth rod was caressing my prostate. I sure was beginning to feel tingly.

"Fuck me, my love," I yelled. "Fuck me as hard as you can. I am so loving this."

Joe didn't need any urging. He was cumming and cumming fast. He increased the speed of his thrusts. His breathing became labored, and then, with a loud scream, I felt his jism shooting high up inside of me. He let his upper torso fall on my chest, and I put my arms around him. He was crying, and his sobs were loud and heavy.

When his breath began to return to normal, he whispered in my ear, "Thank you for loving me. I have loved you since I first laid eyes on you."

"I love you too," I assured him. "Now, let me do the sucking and fucking."

"Take your time, baby. I came at the exact time you did. We'll have to wait a little while."

Thanksgiving dinner, as prepared by Eddie, was not only delicious, but it was warm, cozy and intimate. My dad suggested that we go around the tiny table, and each of us say what we are grateful for.

Eddie said, "A very short time ago, I was lonely and miserable. I basked in my own misery. Now I have a loving family, and a very loving partner. For that I'm grateful."

"Yes," my father added. "I'm grateful to have Eddie in my life, but it wouldn't have been possible if my fantastic son had not loved me enough to do some matchmaking on my behalf. So I'm also grateful for the man he has grown up to be. I love everyone at this table. You are not just family. You are all rocks that I can lean on to stay safe."

Eddie leaned over and gave my father a kiss on his cheek. Joe spoke up next.

"I fell in love with Maury the moment I laid eyes on him. I don't care that it took him longer to love me. I'm just grateful that he eventually did, and that he's willing to share his life with me. I can't ask for anything more"

All eyes turned to me. I hesitated a long time before speaking. I was too choked up to say anything at that moment anyhow. Finally, in a faltering and quaky voice, trying very hard not to cry, I croaked out, "Happiness! I'm grateful for happiness. I'm really, really happy. What is happiness? Happiness for me is everyone at this table."

I turned first to my dad. "Pops," I started out, "you've taken care of me, and nurtured me, all my life. You've always tried to protect me form anything evil in the world, and I have never felt less than safe in your presence. I won't even try to tell you how much I love you. There aren't words strong enough. Thank you for being you, and for all you have done and sacrificed for me."

I turned my eyes to Eddie. "Thank you, Eddie, for lots of things. First and foremost, thank you for making my dad so happy, and for committing yourself to stand by his side for both your lifetimes. I can't tell you enough, how much that means to a son.

"Thank you for turning me on to my true self. Thank you for helping me find my place in the world. I'll never know if you seduced me or I seduced you. It really doesn't matter. I'm grateful for the results, and I owe it all to you.

"Joe, my sweet Joe, I love you so much. I am so grateful that I found you; that we found each other. I can only thank God for the great gift he gave me. It is a privilege to know that we are going to make life's journey together. I can't think of another soul in the universe that I would rather share it with."

Everyone was crying so to lighten the mood, I added, "Joe, promise me that you and I will even share the same medical specialty, so that, not only will we live and play together, but we will work together too. I want to be with you 24-7, so that we never have to wave good-bye, when we go off to work."

Joe raised his wine glass, and said, "Amen to that." Dad and Eddie did the same. As everyone sipped from their wine glasses, I knew that I would never be happier, nor more content than I was at that very moment in time.

The End

Here is a sample from another story you may enjoy:

HANK BROOKS

LONELY CABIN

Murder in My Mind

GAY SUSPENSE EROTICA

One of Steve's required courses was Classical Civilization. He put off taking it until his junior year because he had heard that the only professor who taught the course was supposed to be a total dufus, and a complete bore. Only when he could not put it off any longer, did he enroll in the course. On the evening before his first class, Steve decided to see what he could find out about this universally disliked teacher. The college's web site included a biography of every faculty member. Steve went to the site and clicked on Jeremy Whiting.

Jeremy Whiting, PhD: Dr. Whiting received his doctorate in the study of ancient civilizations from Yale University in 2005. The subject of his thesis was "Rome, After the Fall." It is available in the college library. Dr. Whiting was born in Brooklyn, New York in 1979. He is single. He enjoys, opera, theater, and his favorite pastime is hiking.

The blurb was not accompanied by a picture, and was not very enlightening except for Dr. Whiting's age. Steve expected him to be much older than thirty. He was practically a contemporary. There were more shocks to come.

When Dr. Whiting entered the classroom for the first time, Steve did a double take. Jeremy Whiting was drop-dead gorgeous. He was about six feet tall. He wasn't muscular, but his body was lean and solid. He had soft brown eyes. His brown hair was rather attractively tousled, uncombed but not untidy. He never smiled at the class and Steve was sorry about that. He wanted to know what his smile would be like.

Whiting addressed the class, in a deep baritone voice which would have been rather sexy, except for the fact that he spoke in somewhat of a monotone and droned on forever. Steve realized that it would be an effort to stay awake in his class. By the end of the first hour, Whiting had managed to bore the entire class to a near comatose state. No wonder his status among the student body was so low. Fifteen minutes before the class ended, Steve was dreaming about Brady and his other Saturday night friends. He hadn't taken a single study note, and couldn't tell you what Whiting was talking about. All of Steve's ennui changed during the fourth lecture.

Whiting began to talk about the debauchery and the prevalence of homosexuality in the ancient Greek and Roman civilizations. In spite of his lackluster delivery, the class was all ears. He began to rant and rave about the homosexuals and attributed the fall of both civilizations to the "freaking queers." At last his voice started to become animated as his obvious hatred for homosexuals came out. "If we don't watch out," he spouted venomously, "they will bring down our civilization also."

Steve, and one or two other closeted individuals, squirmed uncomfortably in the already uncomfortable classroom seats. Steve thought that such un-professor-like behavior would end with that lesson, but Whiting kept bringing up the subject in almost every lecture, and displaying his hatred of gays, then and now. In spite of a physical attraction to the professor, Steve detested him. He would have registered a complaint, but he didn't want to out himself. Instead, Steve decided that he would simply murder the good professor. He vowed to commit the perfect crime. To that end, he knew that he had to become Jeremy's friend, without the other students becoming aware of it.

Very few questions were raised in class because very few students knew what the hell Whiting was talking about. Steve refused to allow himself to become distracted by Whiting's droning, and he began to listen carefully to what he had to say. His plan was to jot down meaningful questions. Then at the end of the class, he would linger and approach the professor's desk as he was packing up his attaché case.

"Excuse me, Dr. Whiting," Steve said one day with a lilt in his voice. "May I ask you a question?" Whiting was stunned. This was the first time that any student had ever done this. His experience was that they usually just bolted out of his classroom.

"Why of course, Mr. Mackey," Whiting answered.

"Oh please, call me Steve," Steve said in the friendliest voice he could muster.

"Steve then. What is your question?"

"Well, sir, I'm majoring in engineering, and I was wondering if you could shed some light on how the ancient Romans developed the engineering skills to build the aqueducts? Did they have schools or was it just an innate talent?"

"What a wonderful question. I don't have a definitive answer, but it is a good topic for conversation. If you aren't busy tonight, perhaps you would like to come over to my apartment this evening. We can discuss it over a cup of coffee. I live just a short walk from the campus."

"That would be a singular honor for me, Professor."

That's how it all began. After that, Steve visited Dr. Whiting at least once a week. During those times, he suffered more harangues about the perverts who brought down a great civilization, as well as wonderfully intellectual discussions about the civilizations themselves. Sometimes during the coffee break, Whiting would play his favorite opera arias for them. Other times he would play Broadway tunes.

A strange thing began to happen. Steve began to hate Whiting more and more when he was raving and ranting about queers, but without realizing it, he was falling in love with him when they were conversing about other things, and listening to music. When he wasn't ranting against gays, Jeremy was handsome, warm, caring and loving. He was always concerned about Steve's well-being, and even asked him to call him Jeremy outside the classroom.

Steve learned that Jeremy had no family (murdering him would be easier). He wasn't going anywhere for the upcoming Thanksgiving holiday break. He had no place to go. Steve wasn't going home either, because his parents were going down to Florida to visit his maternal grandparents. Shortly before the Thanksgiving break, he told Jeremy about his love for hiking. Jeremy's ears perked up. He loved hiking also. But then again, Steve already knew that.

"Two years ago, while hiking, I discovered a shack in the forest. I think it had been used by hunters in some long ago time. It was rotting away, but I renovated it and now it has become a retreat for me. I go there to study and do my homework and to get away from the world." He concluded by whispering to Jeremy in a conspiratorial way, "Nobody knows about this place. I've kept it a deep, dark secret. Now you know about it and you are the only one. Would you like to hike with me one day and see it?"

"You honor me," Jeremy said. Then he did something which shocked the hell out of Steve. He embraced Steve and said, "It will be a pleasure to go hiking with you."

"Great," Steve said. "How about at the Thanksgiving break?"

"Perfect," Jeremy agreed.

Steve spent the next two Saturday afternoons, preparing the cottage for the murder of Jeremy Whiting, PhD…

If you enjoyed this sample then look for **Lonely Cabin.**

Also by this Author

Silver Spoon

Ordinary Guy

South Beach Rhapsody

Sensual Bet Rendezvous

Accidentally-in-Love

Lost Emotion

A Commuter's Obsession

Forgiven

Shower Mate

Year-Ender Surprise

The Underdog

Service with Love

The Second Time Around

A Comfortable Sorrow

Personal Choice

Doubtful Heart

As You Are

40th Pleasure

The Love Act

Harry's Trial

About the Author

He was born many years ago in the small town of Brooklyn, NY. His childhood was not a happy one. He was overweight and terrible at all the street games the other kids played. By the time he got to Brooklyn College, he was all slimmed down and smart enough to avoid athletics.

Married at 21, the union produced three fantastic overachievers who subsequently produced five sons between them. He discovered he was gay at a later part of his life. He now lives with his fantastic partner, Leo, in Coconut Creek, Florida.

He has been writing gay stories for a good number of years now and has gained the support of a lot of fans from his written stories. He is also the writer of many more books published by this name, Hank Brooks on Amazon.

From the Author

Check my page on Amazon for Updates and interesting info.

Author Central - http://www.amazon.com/Hank-Brooks/e/B00CKI1Y1Y

If you enjoyed any of my books then please share the love and click like on my books in Amazon.

If you write me a review and send me an email I will send you a free book, or many.
(Just know that these emails are filtered by my publisher.)

Good news is always welcome.

One Last Thing, For Kindle Readers...

When you turn the page, Kindle will give you the opportunity to rate this book and share your thoughts on Facebook and Twitter. If you enjoyed my writings, would you please take a few seconds to let your friends know about it? Because... when they enjoy they will be grateful to you and so will I.

Thank You!

Hank Brooks
hank_brooks@awesomeauthors.org

www.ingramcontent.com/pod-product-compliance
Lightning Source LLC
Chambersburg PA
CBHW071349130626
46556CB00005B/2101